Ellie

Stands Up To The Bully

by Julie Dart

illustrations by MikeMotz.com

ADDITIONAL COPIES ARE AVAILABLE ONLINE AT AMAZON.COM

OR AT MY WEBSITE:

WWW.AUTHORJULIEDART.COM

ISBN: 1478166916
EAN-13: 978-1478166917

First Edition

Printed in the United States of America

Ellie
Stands Up To The Bully
by Julie Dart
illustrations by MikeMotz.com

To Kaitlin and John,
Thank you for allowing me to help you
to believe in yourselves, and thanks for
reminding me to do the same.

Nikki,
Thanks for doing the first edit
and for dreaming with me!

To my dearest Sophia and Julie,
Thank you for inspiring me with your sketches.

And last but not least,
Thank you, Lloyd and Barbie,
for all of your help.

My love, Julie

Julie Dart

TABLE OF CONTENTS

JOEY'S FAVORITE RECIPES
119

A NOTE

FROM THE AUTHOR

Being a mother of two amazing children has been my greatest joy. As my children grew older, I discovered that my passion of passions was to write children's books. I shared that information with Lloyd Russell, my friend and agent.

In 1997, I was pregnant with my son John and riding BART into San Francisco from Fremont. I remembered how I was bullied in middle school and how awful it felt, so I wanted to find a way to help children get through something like that now that I was older. That is when the idea for Ellie came to me.

After speaking to Lloyd, I decided to write and self publish my story of Ellie. I was a little afraid to begin but then my friend, Julie Stark, and her beautiful daughter, Sophia Claire Stark, whom I have named my official "executive assistant," sent some sketches after reading the manuscript. That was the push I needed! Ellie and her friends came to life.

My mother taught me that we must always give back to the community, which is why ten percent of all proceeds from this book will go to Whitney Elementary School in Las Vegas. I felt the need to give to this school when I first saw them on the *Ellen DeGeneres Show*. Why? When we were younger, we had financial hardships of the same kind. I understand their situation and want to help.

All my life, I have wanted to help inspire people to believe in themselves. The book you are reading is one of my dreams come true: for this story to uplift someone and let them know that they can accomplish anything they want to.

I hope that you, too, will feel that there isn't anything you can't do.

I believe in dreams, and I believe in you.

Julie Dart

1

ELLIE'S NEW SCHOOL

Ellie was a yellow elephant who loved to sing and dance. She would put on a silly hat, grab one of her favorite scarves, and run around singing, "Today is a beautiful day. We all can sing and play, and today is a beautiful day."

Her mother thought she was adorable. So did all of her teachers and friends.

"Dance for us again, Ellie!" her friends would say as they watched her dance and sing.

Ellie was especially excited to get up this morning. Today was the first day of second grade at her new school. You see, Ellie's family moved to a new town to live closer to Nana Lillian, her grandmother. Ellie simply adored Nana Lillian. Nana's house was pink with lots of beautiful flowers in the front yard. Ellie looked forward to spending more time with Nana.

When Ellie visited Nana, they baked cookies and played games. Nana had two white cats, Crystalina and Maria. The cats looked like sisters, but they were very different. Crystalina was friendly, but she would scratch if you petted her too long. Maria, the other cat, was shy. Maria was only friendly when you were feeding her.

Ellie liked both of the cats. She asked her mother for a kitty of her own, but her mother said no. Ellie liked to pretend that Crystalina and Maria were her cats. Ellie thought, *Maybe Mom will take me to Nana's house after school. I can give Maria a snack, and maybe she will let me pet her.*

"Almost ready, Ellie?" her mother called from downstairs.

"Almost," Ellie answered as she grabbed her polka-dot backpack and swung it over her shoulder. Before she left her room, Ellie looked at herself in the mirror. She checked herself from head to toe to make sure she looked just right. Ellie gently touched her pink barrette, admiring its blue flower. Mama had fixed it for her at breakfast. Ellie couldn't do her hair by herself yet. Her barrette always seemed to fall out.

Next, Ellie checked her purple-and-white striped dress. It had a beautiful lace collar and ended at her knees. She liked the way it flared out at bottom like a bell. Ellie giggled as she swayed the dress back and forth, saying, "ding, ding, ding" with every swoosh. Ellie looked down at her new black shoes. The shoes were so shiny that she could see her reflection when she looked down.

"Ellie," her mother called again, "come down here, please. It is time to go."

Ellie giggled again and ran downstairs. She loved school! Ellie followed her mother to the car. She got in and put on her seatbelt gently. She did not want to wrinkle her dress.

On the way to school, Ellie asked, "Mama, do you think the kids at school will like me?"

"Oh, yes," said Ellie's mother. "Why wouldn't they? You are the cutest, sweetest girl I have ever seen."

Ellie smiled from the backseat. She put one hand on her

tummy because it felt funny. It felt like butterflies in her tummy, fluttering from all the excitement.

2

THE FIRST DAY SHARING

As Ellie and her mother drove up to the school, Ellie became even more excited. She watched all the children get out of the school bus and their parents' cars.

"Oh, look at all of the children, Mama!" Ellie said.

Her mother parked the car and they held hands as they walked through the parking lot toward school. While they walked, Ellie thought about her day. She wanted to share Nana's lemon bars with her new friends.

Ellie saw a big, yellow, curvy slide on the playground. She couldn't wait to try it out during recess. Ellie thought, *This looks like a really fun school. It is much bigger than my old one.*

They walked into the classroom, and Ellie looked around. The desks were filled with students. *They must be my second-grade classmates*, she thought.

The teacher began to speak. "Good morning. My name is Miss Stacey, and I will be your teacher this year." Ellie noticed that the Miss Stacey wore a yellow dress with pretty purple flowers on it.

"Hello," said Ellie's mother. "This is Ellie, and she is new at this school."

"Well, isn't that wonderful!" said Miss Stacey. "Ellie, I have a nice seat for you, up here close to my desk."

Ellie looked at her new desk. "Thank you, Miss Stacey," Ellie said. She hung up her backpack and hugged her mother goodbye.

"Goodbye, Ellie," said her mother. "I'll be back to pick you up after school. Then we will go to Nana's so you can tell us both about your fun day at school."

"Goodbye, Mama," Ellie said. She sat in her new seat.

The bell rang for class to begin. Miss Stacey shut the door and walked to front of the classroom. A speaker on the wall made a noise, and Ellie heard a man's voice.

"Good morning, students! Welcome to the first day of school at our world famous Star School. My name is Mr. Ray, and I am the principal. If you need anything, just let me or one of your teachers know! We are here to make your learning experience a fun and safe one. Now today for lunch, we have Millie's chili with corn bread and chocolate pudding. Of course, this is served with milk from our world famous Star School dairy."

"Moo!" A fake cow noise came through the speakers, and all the kids laughed. Morning announcements were over.

Miss Stacey said, "Okay, class, let's begin. First, we will go around the room. Please say your name and share one fun activity you did over the summer."

"But we already know each other," a boy said grumpily from the back of the room.

"Well, Nick," said Miss Stacey, "I would still like everyone to introduce themselves so *I* can get to know all of you. And not all of us know everyone in the room. We have a new student named Ellie. Ellie, why don't you begin?"

"Okay," Ellie said. She stood up and took a breath.

"My name is Ellie, and my family moved here to be closer to Nana. This summer, I went to the beach with my cousins, and we built sand castles and looked for shells. It was a lot of fun."

"Very nice, Ellie. Thank you," said Miss Stacey.

Next, Emily stood up. She shared a story about her dog, Cody. Cody had puppies and Emily liked to watch them play and grow.

Emily sat down, and Joey stood up. He told the class that his dad and uncle had built a room onto their house. Joey was able to help them. His favorite part was watching them pour the cement. His dad let him put handprints in the cement before it dried. He even got to sign his name! They put carpet over the cement, but Joey knew that his name and handprints would always be there.

Jessica told the class about her summer day camp. At first, she was scared to go to the camp because she didn't know anyone. But she made friends right away. Then she had a great time tie-dying shirts and having water balloon fights.

3

ELLIE'S NEW FRIENDS

Nick stood up and told the class that he hung out with his older brother, Randy, all summer. "It was fun," Nick said. "We rode our bikes around and stuff."

Ellie thought that Nick looked sad about his summer activity. She thought he tried to make his story sound more interesting. Ellie felt sorry for Nick. She wished she could have invited him to the beach with her.

The rest of the children shared their summer stories. When everyone was finished, it was time for private reading. Ellie went to the bookshelf and grabbed a book with a starfish on the cover. She was so excited about her new school that she could hardly focus on the words below the pictures. Before Ellie reached the last page, the bell rang and it was time for recess. She wanted to play on the yellow curvy slide!

There was a long line when Ellie reached the slide. Other kids were excited to go on the slide, too. Ellie got in the back of the line behind Roger, a smaller boy from her class. Some kids laughed at him, but Ellie thought he was cute.

"Hi," Ellie said to Roger.

"H-h-h-hello," Roger said shyly.

"My name is Ellie."

"M-m-m-my name is R-R-R-Roger, Roger Dilly."

"Nice to meet you, Roger Dilly."

Just then, Nick and his friends walked by. Nick said, "Well, if it isn't Silly Dilly. Nice overalls, peanut!" Nick nudged one of his buddies and they all laughed as they walked away. Roger didn't say anything back to Nick. Ellie wished she knew Roger better so she could make him laugh.

Roger slid down the slide, and then it was Ellie's turn. When she got to the top of the slide, she looked out and saw the whole playground. Ellie gently pushed off the sides of the slide and went down with a *whoosh*.

"Wheee!" Ellie yelled as she flew down the slide. When she reached the bottom, Roger was waiting for her. Ellie let her feet hit the ground. She stood up to fix her dress.

"Hey Roger, do you want to play foursquare?"

"Uh, okay," Roger said, looking down at his feet.

Roger and Ellie played foursquare with Jessica and Joey until the bell rang. It was time to go back to class.

"Hey," Ellie asked as they walked to the classroom, "do you want to sit with me at lunch today? Nana made lemon bars to share with my new friends."

"Sure," Jessica said and looked at Joey to see if it was okay.

Joey nodded yes.

"You too, Roger?"

"Okay. I like lemon bars … I think," said Roger with a smile. They all laughed and joined the line of second graders waiting outside the classroom.

"Come in, children, come in," Miss Stacey said as the door swung open. The children filed into the classroom and sat in their assigned seats. Ellie noticed a list of classroom tasks on the board.

Date on the calendar
Lunch money to the office
Attendance sheet to the office
Light monitor

Miss Stacey said, "As you can see, we have a list of jobs to complete as a class. Each week, I will assign a new person for each job. By the end of the school year, you will all do each job at least once.

"Today, we will start," Miss Stacey continued. "Your names are written on cut-up pieces of paper and mixed in this box. I'm going to pick a name for each job."

Miss Stacey put her hand inside the box and pulled out a piece of paper.

"The first task will be to change the date on the calendar, and the person in charge of that duty this week is ... Joey! Next, I'll choose someone to deliver the lunch money to the office, and that person is Nick. Now we need someone to take the attendance sheet to the office, and that is our newest student, Ellie.

"And last but not least, we have the task of light monitor. This person makes sure the lights are off when we leave the classroom, and that will be Roger.

"These are the jobs for the week and the people who will be in charge of them," Miss Stacey said with a smile. "Oh, I almost forgot. Nick and Ellie, you will walk to the office together each morning to take the lunch money and attendance sheet."

"Oh, great," Nick groaned. "I have to go with her?"

"That's enough, Nick. We all help each other in this classroom," Miss Stacey said calmly.

4

LEMON BARS AND
LUNCH TROUBLE

"Fine," Nick snapped. Ellie could tell that walking to the office with her was *not* fine with Nick. She wondered why he didn't like her.

The rest of the day went quickly. Miss Stacey split the students into teams to see who could put together a puzzle of the United States the fastest. After they finished, they wrote down the name of their favorite state and why they liked it. Ellie had lived in the state of California her whole life. One of the girls, Kelsey, had lived in seven different states. Ellie thought that was amazing.

Ellie wrote about how she loved California when it was sunny, and her mom drove her to the beach. She wrote about how much she loved the ocean, collecting shells and making sand castles. As soon as Ellie finished writing, the bell rang. It was time for lunch! Miss Stacey asked the class to clean up and get their lunches.

Ellie was anxious to sit with her new group of friends. Miss Stacey opened the door. She asked Roger to stay until last whenever the class left the room. That way, he would be sure to turn off the lights. Roger smiled from ear to ear. Ellie could tell he was proud to be the light monitor.

When Ellie left the classroom, she quickly walked to the bathroom to wash her hands before lunch, and then went to the school cafeteria.

"Ellie, come join us," Jessica and Joey called from a table at the back of the room. Roger sat quietly, moving his apple from one hand to the other. The four new friends enjoyed their first lunch together.

"Ellie," Jessica asked, "do you have any brothers or sisters?"

"No, not yet," Ellie said, "but my parents want to have another child now that we've moved to a bigger house."

"That's great," Jessica said.

"Not so great," Joey said loudly. "My little sister drives me crazy."

Jessica laughed. "But she is *so* cute."

"*You* live with her, then!" Joey laughed and nudged Jessica with his elbow.

Ellie began to hand out Nana's lemon bars. All of a sudden, a white glob flew toward their table and landed with a *splat!* It was a bunch of napkins soaked in water. Now their table was a mess. The four friends turned to see who threw it. They were not surprised to see Nick and his friends laughing and giving each other high fives.

Just then, the lunch lady came by and saw the mess. "Who did this? Who made this mess?" she asked in a loud voice. The four friends looked at each other without saying a word. The lunch lady said firmly, "Well, the four of you better clean it up right now."

Jessica and Ellie got paper towels and picked up the pile of mush. They carefully walked over to the garbage can and threw it away. Ellie could hear Nick still laughing. Silently, the four of them sat at their table, unable to eat another bite of their lunches.

Ellie broke the silence. "Hey, let's go play a game," she said.

"I don't feel like playing a game," Jessica said sadly.

"Me neither," said Roger as he pushed his glasses up on his face. Joey just sat, looking down at his feet.

5

ELLIE'S PURPLE SCARF

"Well," said Ellie, "then I'll show you what I do when I'm feeling down. I dance."

"You dance?" asked Jessica.

"Yes, and I sing. It makes me feel better." Ellie pulled out her favorite purple scarf and started to sing a song to her new friends, hoping it would cheer them up.

"Today is a beautiful day. We all can sing and play and today is a beautiful day." She added, "Hurray, hurray, hurray!"

Jessica and Joey started to laugh. Jessica grabbed Joey's hand and they followed after Ellie. Roger slowly followed, too. He skipped and giggled as he caught up with them.

Ellie led them out to the playground. The next thing they knew, a group of kids was following them and singing along. They skipped around the playground several times, singing and laughing.

The yard duty teachers joined in, clapping and singing as the children passed them. The line was long now, and the children sang with Ellie and her friends as they went around the entire playground one last time. When they finally finished, they all stopped to catch their breaths.

"That was fun!" said one of the kids from the back of the line. Just then, the school bell rang and lunch was over. Two kids asked Ellie if they could play with her again tomorrow.

"Sure," Ellie said as she folded up her scarf. She went back to the classroom with Roger, Jessica, and Joey. They all walked into the classroom with big smiles on their faces ... until they saw Nick.

"What are you guys all happy about? We saw you get in trouble with the lunch lady in the cafeteria today," he said with a smirk on his face.

"Yeah," Nick's friend, Thomas, confirmed. "It was funny."

"We were fine," Ellie assured them. "It was only a big pile of napkins. We went and played after lunch and had a great time. That's why we're smiling."

"No one asked you, Smelly Ellie," said Nick. He and Thomas walked to their seats, laughing.

Ellie stood there, unable to move. What Nick said to her was so mean! She felt hurt and frozen. She wanted to run away. She did not want to cry in front of everyone.

Miss Stacey could see that something was wrong. "Ellie, are you okay?" she asked.

Ellie thought she would burst into tears if she spoke, so she nodded her head yes and sat in her seat.

The rest of the day went by slowly. Ellie felt sick to her stomach. This morning she'd had excited butterflies in her stomach, happy to go to her new school. Now she had the sick butterflies flying around.

Ellie was so upset that she wanted school to be over as soon as possible. *Why is Nick so mean to me?* she asked herself. *What have I done to him? Why does he feel this way about me?* She couldn't answer these questions, which made her even more upset.

Ellie wanted to leave school as soon as she could. *Finally!* she thought when the 2:20 bell rang. School was over.

"Remember to bring your decorated star boards tomorrow. Your star boards should have pictures of you on them. They should also tell us about who you are and what you like," Miss Stacey said.

The teacher opened the door for everyone to leave. Ellie got out of her seat and grabbed her backpack so fast that Miss Stacey did not have time to ask about her first day at school.

Ellie walked to where the cars were waiting for pick-up. She was relieved to see her mom's car first in the line. She quickly ran over to the car, opened the door, threw in her backpack, and got in.

"Hey, gorgeous!" her mom said. "How was your first day of school?"

Ellie's eyes filled with tears. "It was great at first. I met three good friends. Roger is kind of shy, Jessica is super sweet, and Joey has a little sister who drives him crazy.

"But then … but then …" Ellie tried to talk, but the words couldn't come out. She burst into tears—the tears she had held back since Nick had called her that name.

6

SAD INSIDE

"Oh my," said Ellie's mother. She drove down the street and stopped in front of the small park on the corner. Ellie's mom parked and got out. She climbed in the backseat with Ellie.

"Now, now," said her mother, "there isn't anything that we can't fix. What is it, Els?" She put her arm around Ellie and offered her a tissue.

Ellie blew her nose, which was red from crying. "I was playing with my friends, and we were having a good time. Then, at lunch, this boy, Nick, and his friends threw a bunch of wet napkins on our lunch table.

"The lunch lady didn't see them throw it. She just saw the mess and yelled at us to clean it up, so we did. My friends felt sad because of that. I decided to pull out my scarf and sing to them to make them feel better."

"And did it work?" asked her mother.

"Yes," Ellie said, smiling. "You should have seen us, Mama! We were singing the song and dancing in a line across the schoolyard. Then other kids came and joined in, too! It was so much fun."

Her mother said, "That sounds wonderful. Then why the sad face, sweetheart?"

"When we came back from lunch," Ellie sniffled, "Nick said that he saw us clean up the mess. He thought it was funny. He asked why we looked happy after that.

"I said we were singing and dancing, and it made us happy." Ellie began to cry again. "Then he said, 'No one asked you, Smelly Ellie.'" Tears flooded Ellie's eyes, causing her nose to turn red all over again.

Ellie's mom sat quietly with her for a while. She said, "Ellie, you know that people are mean because they are sad inside. This Nicholas boy…"

"Nick, his name is Nick, and he is *so* mean, Mama!"

"I know, sweetheart, and it is very hard to be kind or understanding to someone who is mean to us. But Ellie, you know that deep down inside Nick is sad, and *that's* why he is doing this."

Ellie remembered when Nick shared his summer activity. He didn't seem happy about his summer break. "Yes, Mama, I know, but what he said still hurts my feelings," she admitted.

"I know it does," her mother said. "No one likes to be called names. Why don't we go by Nana's on the way home? You can see Crystalina and Maria. That might cheer you up. And I know Grandma would love to see you."

"Okay," Ellie said. "Oh, Mama, I need to find some pictures of myself. Miss Stacey said that we are all special. She wants us to decorate a poster board with our pictures because we are all stars. Miss Stacey said we all shine in our own way. That is why the boards are called star boards."

Ellie's mother said, "I'm sure Nana has some great pictures of you. Let's go see."

Ellie's face lit up. She couldn't wait to see Nana. Her smile got even bigger when they walked in the door and smelled the cookies Nana was baking.

"Hello, Nana!" Ellie yelled with excitement. "Those cookies sure smell good!"

"Well, hello there, dolly. How is my little granddaughter doing today?"

"Good," Ellie said, "and even better now that I'm here."

Nana asked, "Is that because you're excited to see *me* or excited to eat the cookies?"

"Both!" Ellie laughed as she ran to Nana and gave her a big hug.

Nana hugged Ellie back and kissed her on the head. "Let's get you some cookies, shall we?"

Ellie smiled and nodded yes as they walked into the kitchen.

7

STAR BOARD

Ellie's mother was already in the kitchen taking Nana's cookies out of the oven. Her mother said, "Mama, you have outdone yourself today. These smell delicious!"

"Hey, Nana," Ellie said, "may I take one of the cookies to my teacher tomorrow?"

"Sure," said Nana. "I think your teacher would like that."

"Tell Nana about your day," Ellie's mother said. Ellie told Nana about her teacher and how nice she was. She told her about the morning announcements and the cow sound that made everyone laugh. Then she told Nana about her new friends, and how they sang and danced together at lunch.

She also told Nana about Nick. When Ellie talked about Nick, she had to put her cookie down. She was getting that sick feeling in her stomach again. Nana said that when she was Ellie's age, a girl at her school picked on her, too.

"What did you do, Nana?"

"Well," Nana said, "I told my parents everything the girl said and did to me. It's important to share what people are doing to you so your parents understand. They can help you talk to the teacher or principal at the school. Your parents and teacher can help you figure out how to handle the situation."

Ellie said, "I did that today, and it helped. Mama said people who do mean things are usually sad inside. That is why they do mean things."

"Your mama is right," said Nana. "This boy, Nick, has something sad inside him. That's why he is being so mean."

Ellie hugged her and said, "Thank you, Nana!"

"You're welcome," Nana said.

Ellie skipped to the other room to check on the kitties. She felt much better about Nick. She even told Maria, Nana's kitten, about him. Ellie felt that Maria understood every word. Or maybe it was the delicious snacks Nana gave her to feed Maria. *One can never tell with kitties*, Ellie thought, giggling to herself.

After finishing her last cookie, Ellie looked through the pictures Nana had gathered for her star board. Ellie had not seen some of these pictures before. Some of the pictures were silly and made her laugh.

In one picture, Nana was giving Ellie a bath in the kitchen sink! Ellie could not believe she was ever that small. In another picture, she was baking a cake with Nana. Ellie wore a big chef's hat that went over one of her eyes. Ellie recognized her favorite cake right away. It was confetti.

In another picture, Ellie played with her cousin, Erin. They were dressed like pretty princesses. Then there was one with Ellie and her cousin wearing the same pajamas. Ellie giggled when she saw the next picture. She was holding Crystalina in the palm of her hand. Nana laughed, too.

"Which pictures would you like to use for your star board?" Nana asked Ellie.

"Let's use the one of you and me making the cake; that's my favorite. And how about the one of me dressed up like a princess? And the one holding Crystalina the day you brought her home."

Ellie began to decorate her star board by pasting on the pictures and drawing frames around each one. She wrote words like "dancing," "singing," and "animals" so that everyone would see the things she liked. Ellie finished the board with her name across the top in purple marker.

"Wow," said her mother, "that is a beautiful star board!"

"Thank you, Mama!"

That night, while lying in her bed, Ellie thought about her day. She thought about her friends and sharing Nana's lemon bars. She thought about how nice Miss Stacey was. She also thought about her mother and Nana and how they always made her feel better, no matter what.

Then she thought about Nick and sighed. "I hope he's nice to me tomorrow," Ellie whispered as she pulled her cozy covers up to her nose. She gazed at the stars from her bedroom window.

8

ELLIE'S CLASS JOB

The next day, Ellie woke up to the smell of French toast and her mom's coffee.

"Good morning, sunshine," her mom said when Ellie skipped into the kitchen. "How did you sleep?"

"Great! I'm excited to give Miss Stacey my star board!"

"Oh, I'm glad to hear that, Els. I'm sure Miss Stacey will love it as much as I do." Mama set the French toast in front of her. Ellie grinned when she saw that her French toast was cut in a heart shape.

"Mama, thanks!"

"You're welcome, sweetheart. Now, let's see if you can eat it all up before school. It's almost time to go."

"Okay, and don't forget the cookie from Nana. I'm going to give it to my teacher today."

"Okay, I'll put it in your lunch."

Ellie finished eating and went to her room to get ready. She dressed quickly and picked up her star board. Today felt like a new day for Ellie. *Maybe Nick will be in a better mood*, she thought.

"Ready?" her mom asked as she held out Ellie's lunch.

"Yes!" Ellie said, holding her star board in one hand and grabbing her lunch with the other.

At school, Ellie saw many of her classmates with their star boards in hand. On her friend Roger's board, she saw a man standing next to a racehorse. Ellie noticed a little boy sitting on top of the horse. She thought the boy must be Roger when he was little.

Jessica walked into the classroom after Ellie. She had a lot of animals on her star board. There were cats, dogs, and a turtle. Right behind Jessica was Joey. He had a lot of baseball pictures on his board.

"Okay," said Miss Stacey, "let's take our seats. One at a time, I'll have you come up here and share your star board. But first, I need Nick and Ellie. Please take the lunch order and the attendance sheet to the office."

Ellie heard two boys laughing in the back of the room. Her stomach sank. She knew that Nick and his friend, Thomas, were laughing at her. *Remember*, she thought, *Mama said he was mean because he's sad inside.*

"Okay, you two," said Miss Stacey, "come get these and take them to the office. Then we can start sharing the wonderful star boards you brought in today."

Ellie stood and gave Miss Stacey the cookie Nana had made. "This is for you, Miss Stacey. Nana baked it yesterday."

"Well, it looks yummy. I will eat it on my break. Thanks, Ellie."

Miss Stacey handed Ellie the attendance sheet. Nick came up and took the lunch money envelope from Miss Stacey. He also grabbed the attendance sheet from Ellie's hand. Before Ellie could do anything, he stormed out the door.

Ellie took a deep breath. She couldn't tell whether her feelings were hurt or if she was mad at Nick. Either way, she followed him out the door toward the office. Nick was already down the hall when Ellie came out of the class-room.

"Hey, wait up!" Ellie called. She picked up her pace. "We're *both* supposed to take the attendance sheet, Nick."

"Oh yeah? Well, I'm already at the office. I don't need your help, Smelly."

Ellie's feelings were hurt once again. *Why is he so mean to me?* she thought. "Fine," Ellie said. She tried to hold back her tears so Nick would not see them. "Take them to the office by yourself, then." Ellie turned and walked back to the classroom.

"Where's Nick?" Miss Stacey asked.

"He went to the office by himself," Ellie said sadly. She took a seat at her desk.

The door flew open. It was Nick.

"Nick," Miss Stacey said, "taking the attendance sheet out of Ellie's hands wasn't polite. I need you to tell her that you're sorry."

"What?" Nick said in annoyance. "I didn't do anything to her."

"I saw you do it," said Miss Stacey. "Taking the attendance sheet and the lunch money to the office is a team effort. You were supposed to walk with Ellie. Now please say you're sorry."

Nick's face turned redder by the second. "Sorry," he said between clenched teeth. He turned quickly and stomped back to his desk.

Ellie was not sure how she felt. She was glad Miss Stacey helped her stick up for herself. At the same time, she felt afraid of Nick. He had gotten in trouble, and he seemed very upset.

9

THE SLIDE

Miss Stacey said, "Now we will start off our morning by sharing our star boards. Let's begin with Roger."

Roger stood up and walked to the front of the room. "This is my star board. I have pictures of my uncle's horses on it. My uncle is a jockey."

"Can you tell the class what a jockey is?" asked Miss Stacey.

"Sure," Roger said, ever so politely. "A jockey is a person who rides the horse in a horse race. My uncle is super fast. He has won more than fifteen races. I have pictures of my uncle on my star board, and pictures of other horses. I want to be a jockey when I grow up."

One by one, everyone in the class shared their star boards. Jessica had animals all over her board because she wanted to be a veterinarian one day.

Joey wanted to be a baseball player. His board had pictures of his Little League baseball team. Ellie liked the photo of him smiling and holding up a ball. He and his father caught the ball at a professional game.

"Nick," said Miss Stacey, "it's your turn to share your star board."

"I don't have one," he said from the back of the room.

"Well, everyone has to do one," said Miss Stacey. "Maybe you could bring some pictures from home tomorrow. I will help you paste them on your board."

"Okay," Nick said in a low voice.

"Well," said Miss Stacey, "it looks like Ellie is the last student to share her star board. Come on up here, Ellie."

Ellie grabbed her board and walked to the front. As soon as she looked at all her classmates, she became nervous. It was a new thing, to stand up in front of the class. When she started sharing her board, she began to relax.

"This is Nana and me." Ellie pointed to the confetti cake picture. "We're baking a cake. I love to bake with her. Over here is a picture with my cousin, Erin. We like to dance in our princess costumes. And here is a picture of Nana's kitty, Crystalina. I love Nana's kitties, but I am not allowed to have my own yet."

"Wonderful," said Miss Stacey. "Thanks, Ellie. And thank you all for sharing your star boards. You all did such a great job with them! I will hang them in the classroom while you're out at recess. Good work, everyone," she said.

"Now it is time to line up for recess. Roger, please be the last person in line so you can turn off the lights."

Roger jumped out of his seat and headed for the end of the line.

On the playground, Ellie and her friends went to play foursquare. Other kids were already playing, so Roger, Jessica, Joey and Ellie got in line and waited their turn. They were talking about their star boards when Nick and some other kids approached the line. They pushed their way to the front, upsetting the others who were waiting their turn.

"Hey, no cuts!" said Jessica. "We were here first."

Nick mocked Jessica, using a baby voice. "Hey, no cuts. We were here first."

"Well, we *were*," said Jessica.

"Yeah? Well, *we* are here now, so get out of here and go sing and dance with Smelly Ellie over there."

Nick imitated Ellie with the baby voice. "I wuv cooking and baking with my Nana. Ha ha!" Nick laughed. "The only good thing about your pictures was that your dumb baking hat covered half of your ugly face."

This time, Ellie really felt sick to her stomach. She wanted to leave. She ran as fast as she could to the office.

10

STOMACHACHE

When Ellie got to the office, she burst into tears. The office lady jumped out of her seat to console her.

"Oh my," she said. "What is wrong, sweetheart?"

"I don't feel well. I-I-I want to go home."

"Okay, okay," said the lady. "Let's just see what's going on here."

The office door flew open, and there stood Jessica, Joey, and Roger, panting. Her three friends ran to see if Ellie was okay.

"Children, can I help you?" asked the office lady.

"We're checking on Ellie. Is she okay?"

"She is not feeling well. I'm going to call her mother so that Ellie can be picked up."

Her three friends looked at each other. "Ellie," asked Jessica, "are you sure you want to go home?"

"Y-y-yes," Ellie said, still crying and holding her stomach.

"Okay, then," Jessica said, "we'll see you tomorrow." Ellie nodded and waved goodbye.

The office lady took Ellie to the nurse's station and had her lie down on a cot. "Just rest until your mom comes, Ellie. I'll be right here at my desk if you need anything."

"Okay," sobbed Ellie. *My stomach does hurt*, Ellie thought, *and I do feel sick*. "I want Mommy," Ellie whispered to herself. She thought that if she said it out loud, her mother would magically hear her and come faster.

Ellie lay there waiting, sobbing a little. A few minutes later, she heard the door open.

"Hi, I'm Ellie's mother. She isn't feeling well?"

"She's right in here," said the office lady.

"H-h-h-hi, Mama. I don't feel very good."

Ellie's mother said, "Okay, let's get your things and go."

"Thank you," she said to the office lady as they left.

"I hope she feels better soon," said the office lady.

Ellie was silent all the way home. She wanted to go home and get into bed. *I never want to go back to school ever again*, she thought.

"All right," said Ellie's mother, "let's get you in the house and you can lie down."

Ellie said in a solemn voice, "I just want to go to bed, Mama."

Her mother walked Ellie up the stairs. Ellie slipped off her shoes, jumped into bed, closed her eyes and pretended to sleep. Mama kissed her on the forehead. She gently closed Ellie's door behind her.

11

MEASLES

In her bed, Ellie thought of ways to pretend she was sick. She wanted her mother to let her stay home from school. *I could put red dots all over my face ... Mama would think I have the measles*, she thought.

Ellie quietly made her way over to her desk. She tried not to make a noise, so her mother would not know she was up. Ellie slowly opened the desk drawer and found a red pen.

She went to the mirror and drew red dots all over her face and hands. Then she marked her arms and neck and legs until she had red dots everywhere. She put the pen back in the drawer and quietly tiptoed back to her bed.

Ellie heard the phone ring, and her mother was talking to someone. Her mother hung up the phone and walked upstairs. When she opened the door, Ellie was lying in bed with her eyes closed.

Mama placed her hand softly on Ellie's shoulder. "Ellie," she said, "I need to talk to you about something."

"Huh?" Ellie said, trying to sound sleepy.

"That was Miss Stacey on the phone."

"Really?" said Ellie.

"Your friend Jessica told her that Nick was very rude to you at recess today. Is that true?"

Ellie was not good at lying to her mother, but she tried anyway. "N-n-no. I just felt sick and wanted to come home."

"Ellie," said her mother, "you mustn't lie about being sick. Did you go to the office because Nick hurt your feelings?"

"No, Mama, I *am* sick," Ellie declared. "Look, I even have red dots all over my face and hands."

Ellie's mother looked closely at the red dots and shook her head. "Ellie, you and I both know that those are marks from a red pen. Now, I can help you solve this, but we need to talk about it."

"Oh Mama, can't you just tell the school that I have measles? Pretty please? I'll read ten books a day, I promise. Please, Mama, *please*. Don't make me go back to school!" Ellie sobbed loudly into her pillow.

"Ellie, I know this feels impossible to solve right now. Listen, you have friends and family and your teacher. We all want to help you." Ellie looked up from her pillow. Once again, her nose was bright red, and her messy hair fell out of the barrette.

"Mama, it *is* Nick. He is so mean! He's the meanest person I've ever met. He's meaner than the bad people I see on TV, Mama."

"I know, Ellie. There must be something really bad in his life that makes him act this way. Please, tell me exactly what happened today."

Ellie told her mother about her morning. She said that Nick and his friend laughed, and how Nick grabbed the attendance sheet from Ellie and ran to the office. She told her mother that Nick called her Smelly Ellie again.

Mama listened quietly. Ellie said that Miss Stacey

made Nick say he was sorry, and that Nick looked angry about it. She even told her mother about foursquare, and how he made fun of Ellie and her star board in a baby voice.

Ellie's mother said, "I can see why you are so upset. Those are really mean things to do and say. Why don't you let me talk to Miss Stacey about this? Then, young lady, we'll get you into the bath. We need to wash off those measles!"

"Okay," Ellie said, managing a giggle.

Ellie heard her mother talking to Miss Stacey on the phone. "I am very concerned about the way Nick is treating Ellie, Miss Stacey," Mama said. "I want Ellie to feel comfortable about going back to school. Let's see what we can do to make that happen.

"Yes, I will tell Ellie that you understand, and that you will help her. Thank you, Miss Stacey." Mama hung up the phone.

12

ELLIE GETS HELP

"Okay, Ellie, let's get you in the tub," Mama said.

"Do we have any bubble bath left?"

"I think so. Let's go check." Ellie's mother got the pink bottle of bubble bath and poured it into the tub. Ellie got in as the tub filled with water. She played with the bubbles and made a cake.

"Hey, Mama, it's a birthday cake for you. Blow out the candles!" Ellie's mother blew and tiny bubbles flew onto Ellie's head. She looked like she had big, fuzzy hair.

"There's a pretty picture," said Ellie's mother.

Ellie giggled. She loved bubble baths. They made her feel silly and she could play pretend.

"Did you get the red dots off?" her mother asked.

Ellie looked at her hands. "Yes. Are there any left on my face?"

"No," her mother said. "I think you are now one hundred percent cured of the measles."

Ellie laughed. Mama handed Ellie her ducky robe. It had pictures of yellow ducks all over the blue robe.

"Looks like you worked up an appetite in the bathtub. Are you hungry for dinner yet?"

Ellie realized how hungry she was. She had not eaten anything since the French toast at breakfast. Mama pulled out the chair for Ellie to sit in. She put one of Ellie's favorite meals on the table: vegetable soup and a grilled cheese sandwich.

"Yay," Ellie said. Her mother sat next to her and they began to eat.

When they were done, Ellie's mother said, "You know, Els, you have to go to school tomorrow."

"I know, Mama, but what should I do if Nick is mean to me again?"

"Miss Stacey said she was going to talk to the class today about bullying, so that should help."

"What does bullying mean?" Ellie asked.

"Bullying is when someone picks on another person by calling them names or trying to push them around."

"Nick never tried to push me, Mama."

"I know, Ellie, but there are two kinds of bullying. One kind is when people use words, and another kind is when someone tries to hurt you physically. Neither one is okay. Miss Stacey and the principal, Mr. Ray, are going to help you in any way they can."

"Okay, Mama. I will give it another try."

"Good job, sweetheart. I am very proud of you. Now let's talk about what you can do if Nick comes near you. If Nick says, 'Hey, Smelly Ellie,' what could you say or do to make yourself feel better?"

"Well," said Ellie slowly, "I could walk away."

"Yes, you could," said her mother.

"Or I could tell him that I didn't like what he was saying and that it was mean."

"Yes, that might work."

"I could remind myself that he says those things because he is sad inside, even if it doesn't show on the outside."

"True," said Ellie's mother. "Miss Stacey wants to make sure that you tell her about any mean things Nick says to you, no matter how small."

"But Mama, isn't that tattle telling?"

"No, Ellie. If someone does or says something to hurt you on purpose, it isn't tattle telling to let your teacher know."

"Okay, Mama. I will try my best." Ellie yawned.

"Good for you," her mom said. "All right, young lady, let's end the day with a nice story. Why don't you pick one out, and I'll be up there in a minute to read it to you before bed."

Ellie hopped off the chair and skipped over to the stairs. In her room, she looked through her books and found the one she wanted her mother to read. "Aha," she said. "This one will be perfect."

The book was called *The Adventures of Jimmy and His Red Jacket*. This was one of Ellie's favorite books. It was about a boy whose family did not have much money. One day, Jimmy went to a thrift store with his father and got a red jacket as a gift.

Jimmy began to think that the jacket was magic. Every time Jimmy made a wish with his red jacket on, the wish would come true. It turns out that the jacket wasn't magical after all. Jimmy thought such amazing thoughts that good things happened to him.

Ellie really liked this story. She never tired of hearing how Jimmy's life was wonderful once he started thinking happy thoughts. Ellie's mother read her the entire book, but before she could say "the end," Ellie was fast asleep.

13

PURPLE OVERALLS
AND PINK TENNIS SHOES

The next morning, Ellie woke to the sound of the blender. "Smoothies!" she said with a smile. Ellie put on her ducky robe and went to the kitchen. Her mother was making strawberry smoothies.

"Good morning, young lady," her mother said as Ellie sat at the kitchen table.

"Good morning, Mama," Ellie said.

"You look like you slept well."

"Yes, I did. I dreamed that I had Jimmy's red jacket."

"You did?"

"Yes, and I ran around the playground sharing it with Roger, Joey, Jessica, and even Nick."

"Wow," said Ellie's mother, "that sounds like a great dream."

"It was! Mama, I was thinking about how people are mean because they have something sad inside of them."

"Yes?"

"I'm going to look at Nick that way today."

"What do you mean, Ellie?" her mother asked.

"I'm not going to see Nick as mean and scary. I'm going to look at him as a very sad boy who is doing mean things."

"Somehow, that sounds like it might help you," said Ellie's mom.

"Then I won't take it so seriously. I will remember that he is only being mean because he is sad."

"That's great!" said her mother. "Oh, it's already time to go! Are you done with your smoothie?"

"I'm going to wear my purple overalls and pink tennis shoes today."

"Okay. And why is that?"

"Because wearing that outfit makes me happy. Want to know why?"

"Yes," her mother said, laughing, "I do want to know why that outfit makes you happy."

"Purple and pink are my favorite colors, and wearing them makes me happy."

Her mother said, "Okay, you wear that outfit today."

Ellie dressed quickly and brushed her teeth in record time.

"Let's go, Mama!" Ellie said. She grabbed her lunch and her backpack.

"Well," said her mother, "you sure are on time today."

Ellie said, "I'm actually excited to go back to school today."

They drove to Ellie's school. "Tra la la, tra la la," sang Ellie as they drove.

When they arrived, her mother said, "I would like to walk with you to your classroom. Is that okay?"

"Sure, Mama. Let's go." Ellie jumped out of the car and took her mother's hand. When they walked into the classroom, Miss Stacey's eyes lit up.

"Hello, Ellie, *so* good to have you back. Are you feeling better?"

"Yes," said Ellie, "much better." She giggled, thinking of her measles the day before.

"Have a seat, Ellie. We are just about to begin."

Ellie gave her mother a hug, hung up her backpack, and went to her seat. Just then, Thomas and Nick walked in. Nick stopped quickly when he saw Ellie, and Thomas bumped into him.

"Watch it," Nick yelled at Thomas.

"Sorry, gosh," Thomas said. They both took their seats in the back.

There was a loud beep that meant the morning announcements were coming on. "Hello, students, I am Mr. Ray, your principal here at the world famous Star School. Today for lunch, we're having corn dogs, carrot sticks, and peanut butter. As always, this great lunch includes milk from our world famous Star School dairy."

"Moooo," the fake cow said. Once again, the children laughed, and so did Miss Stacey.

Miss Stacey said, "Okay, let's have Nick and Ellie run the attendance sheet and the lunch money to the office. When they return, I'll break you into groups and have you do a word search. Whichever group finishes the word search first gets to line up first for lunch."

"Yes!" Joey said, smiling at Jessica.

"Ellie and Nick, can you please come up here and take these to the office?" They both walked up to the teacher's desk. Miss Stacey handed Nick the envelope with the lunch money. She handed Ellie the attendance sheet.

"Okay, see you back here in a couple minutes," Miss Stacey said.

14

ELLIE STANDS UP

Nick took his envelope, threw open the door and ran down the hallway to the office. Ellie watched him and thought about her conversation with her mom. She remembered that Nick was sad about something.

Suddenly, something happened inside Ellie. She knew that she was in charge of her feelings. She talked to herself out loud. "Ellie, you are happy, and Nick is sad. Don't let him make you feel unhappy, too. You have Nana, Mama, Miss Stacey, and your friends to help you. You can do this, Ellie!"

Ellie would not let what Nick said bother her ever again. *He's just a sad boy. There's nothing to be afraid of.* Now Ellie almost felt sorry for Nick. She wished she knew what he was sad about so she could help him.

As Ellie opened the office door, Nick came flying out, saying, "You're too slow, Smelly."

Ellie stared at him, but this time it didn't hurt her feelings. Ellie just felt a little annoyed with Nick. She let out a deep sigh and shook her head.

"Well, look who we have here," said the office lady. "Don't you look better today!"

"Thanks. Here's the attendance sheet."

"Thank you so much, Ellie, and welcome back."

"Thank you," Ellie said. "Have a nice day."

"You too," said the office lady.

Ellie left the office and started back to the classroom. When she was a few doors away, she saw Miss Stacey standing in the doorway with Nick.

"Is everything all right?" Miss Stacey asked Ellie.

"Everything is great, Miss Stacey."

"Okay, let's begin our word search," Miss Stacey said in a cheery voice.

They were divided into six groups of four students each. Ellie and Roger were in a one group, and Jessica and Joey were in another. Ellie and Roger did a good job of helping each other. Ellie found the word "principal," while Roger found "ruler" and "crossing guard."

They had only two words to go when they heard "Done!" from across the room. It was Joey and Jessica's group. "Okay, let me have a look," Miss Stacey said.

Joey handed her their word search. "It looks like table five is the winner. Good job, everyone! Now please go back to your seats. The bell is about to ring for recess. Table five, you may line up first." The table five kids happily headed to the door.

"Everyone else, you may come and line up. Roger," Miss Stacey asked, "would be so kind as to be the last one out, so you can shut off the lights?"

"Sure," Roger said. Roger and Ellie went to the end of the line, where Nick and Thomas stood.

"Hey, Shorty and Smelly," Nick mumbled. He and Thomas laughed.

One by one, the children left the classroom until they were all outside. Roger smiled as he turned off the lights and closed the door.

"Hey Ellie!" Jessica called. She came running over. "Are you okay?"

"Yes, I'm okay. Sorry about yesterday."

"You were pretty upset about what Nick said, huh?" asked Joey.

Jessica nudged him as a way of saying "drop it."

"Yes, I was. I talked to my mom, and she said that people are bullies if they're sad about something. Otherwise, they would be too happy to want to hurt anyone. When she told me that, I wasn't scared of Nick anymore. I feel sorry for him, that's all."

Jessica said, "Well, we are glad to have you back. Do you want to play on the slide with us?"

"Sure," said Ellie. They walked to the big yellow slide and took turns sliding down. First went Roger, then Jessica, then Joey, and finally, Ellie.

"Wheee," Ellie said, laughing. She was so happy to be playing with her friends. Suddenly, Nick and Thomas walked up.

"What are you playing on that dumb slide for? That slide is for babies. You must be babies," Nick said, laughing.

15

ELLIE'S DANCE

"No, we are not babies, Nick," said Ellie, full of confidence. "We just like slides."

"No one asked you, Smell…"

Before he could say it, Ellie said, "Smelly Ellie. Gosh, Nick, are those the only mean words you know?"

Nick just stood there, shocked. So did the other kids.

"I mean, really, aren't there any other words you can come up with? So we can hear something different?"

Nick did not say a word, and neither did Thomas. They were amazed that Ellie did not cry and run away.

"Honestly, Nick," Ellie continued, "sometimes I think you are just bored. When you see us having fun, you have to try and ruin it for us. But we have better things to do than to sit around and listen to you call me names.

"Come on," Ellie said to her friends. Roger, Joey, and Jessica followed Ellie as she walked to the middle of the playground.

"Oh, my gosh!" said Jessica. "That was amazing, Ellie!"

"Yeah, look at him," said Joey. "He's still standing there. He doesn't know what to do."

Roger went to Ellie and put his hand on her shoulder. "Way to go Ellie. Way to go."

Ellie giggled. "It's no big deal. When you realize that someone is sad inside and that's why they say mean things, it really makes you feel sorry for them. I am not afraid of Nick after all!"

"What do you want to do now?" Joey asked.

"I have an idea," Ellie said, and she pulled out her purple scarf. They all began to laugh.

"Yes, Ellie," Jessica said, "sing for us."

Ellie began to sing, "Today is a beautiful day. We all can sing and play and today is a beautiful day. Hurray, hurray, hurray!"

Other children joined in as Ellie and her friends sang and danced in a line around the playground. The yard duty teachers clapped as the children danced and sang their wonderful song. Ellie glanced around, but she did not see Nick and his friends.

Ellie knew that from now on, she would not be afraid of Nick. She had her friends, her family, and her teacher, and that was all she needed. She was going to be okay.

When the children heard the school bell ring, they danced and sang all the way back to the classroom. "Today is a beautiful day. We all can sing and play and today is a beautiful day. Hurray, hurray, hurray!"

THE END

APPENDIX

JULIE'S RESOURCE GUIDE

Remember, it is not a weakness to ask for help. It takes strength to ask for help.

Please reach out to one or more of these resources until you feel empowered to move forward. I know you can make it through this—I did, and so can you! And who knows? Maybe you are going through this to help other people, as I have done.

Children
Please tell parents, teachers, the principal, and friends. Keep telling until someone helps.

Remember that the person bullying you is not a happy person. Happy people don't hurt other people. It may not seem like it from the outside, but inside they are hurting.

If you are watching someone who is being bullied and you do not know how to help, simply step away. Bullies like an audience. If they don't have people watching, they often stop.

Parents

It is important to empower children during this time. If they have an activity they are good at, have them spend time doing at that to improve their self-esteem. Reach out to help others. When we help others, we become empowered.

Resources

My favorite resource is from Boys Town®. This site is not just for boys; it is family oriented and has all the help you need. Their organization includes the following resources, and their phone line is open 24 hours. I have called the 800 number and they have the most caring and loving people there to speak to.

www.boystown.org
1-800-448-3000, open 24/7

Other sites

www.parenting.org
www.yourlifeyourvoice.org
www.projectcornerstone.org
www.mayoclinic.com
www.athinline.org
www.thetrevorproject.org

Hotline

1-866-488-7386

My blessings are with you,

THE CAST

AND THEIR FAVORITE RECIPES

MEET ELLIE

Age: 7 years old

Grade: 2nd

Eyes: blue

Hair: pink

Favorite Color:
Ellie has two favorite
colors: pink and purple

Favorite activity:
Dancing, singing, reading, writing,
and being with her friends and family.

Favorite place to go on vacation:
The ocean!

What does she want to be when she grows up:
A teacher or an author.

Pets:
Not yet, but she wants a puppy or a cat; in the meantime she loves her Nana's kitties, Crystalina and Maria.

Siblings:
Not yet, but hopes her mother and father will want one soon

What school do you attend:
Star School.

Where we you born:
Paris

ELLIE'S

FAVORITE RECIPES

SMOOTHIES

In a Blender:

2 apples (cleaned, cored and cut into 4 pieces)
2 bananas (peeled and broken in half)
1 cups of frozen mangos
1 cup of water

Blend well and serve.

Enjoy!

SMOOTHIES

In a Blender:

2 peaches (clean and cut up into f pieces and remove seed)
1 banana (peeled and cut in half)
2 oranges (peeled and cut into 4 pieces)
1 cup of frozen peaches
1 cup of water

Blend well and serve.

Enjoy!

SMOOTHIES

In a Blender:

1 cup of raspberries (rinse well)
2 bananas (peeled and cut in half)
1 cup of crushed ice
1 cup of Water

Blend well and serve.

Enjoy!

ROLLED SANDWICH

White or Wheat Bread
1 can of Tuna
Mayonnaise
Romaine lettuce
Rolling pin

Directions:

Drain water or oil from tuna and mix with mayonnaise
(desired amount) in a bowl and set to side.

Take a clean cutting board and cut crust off of bread.

Taking rolling pin and flatten bread as thin
as you can get without breaking.

Take tuna and spread evenly.

Place cleaned romaine lettuce evenly on top of tuna.

Then grab once side of the bread and begin to roll.

You can then cut it in half or leave it
just like that and begin to eat.

Enjoy!

ROLLED SANDWICH

White or Wheat Bread
Creamy Peanut Butter
Strawberry Jelly
Rolling pin

Directions:

Take a clean cutting board and cut crust off of bread.

Taking rolling pin and flatten bread as thin
as you can get without breaking.

Spread creamy peanut butter evenly
then do the same with jelly.

Then grab once side of the bread and begin to roll.

You can then cut it in half or leave it
just like that and begin to eat.

Enjoy!

CHICKEN BURRITOS

1 can of pinto beans
1 cup of Enchilada sauce (mild)
1 chicken breast
½ cup of shredded cheddar cheese
Tortillas

Directions:

Cook chicken in pan about 4 min on each side
(make sure it's not pink in middle).

Cut chicken into bean size pieces.

Drain pinto beans and add to chicken in a pan.

Add enchilada sauce and cheese and heat until warm.

Heat tortilla and a roll it up with yummy mix inside
and you are all set.

Enjoy!

SPINACH SALAD

1 bag Spinach
1 can Garbanzo Beans
Feta Cheese
Lemon

Directions:

In a bowl, place clean spinach leaves.

Drain garbanzo beans and place them on top of salad.

Place ½ cup of feta cheese on top of salad.

Take a clean lemon and slice in half.

Remove seeds and squeeze half of the lemon on top of salad.

Gently mix and serve.

Enjoy!

OATMEAL WITH APPLES

1 cup Quaker Oats
2 cups of diced apples
1 tbsp of brown sugar
½ teaspoon of vanilla extract
2 1/2 cups 2 % milk
2 tbsp honey
1 tbsp of cinnamon

Directions:

Put everything in a Crockpot

Cook on low for 4-5 hours or until sides are golden brown.

Enjoy!

CUCUMBER SANDWICH

Wheat Bread
Cream Cheese
Cucumber

Directions:

Thinly slice a clean cucumber. Set to side.

Take two slices of wheat bread.

Spread cream cheese on each side of bread.

Place desired amount of cucumber inside.

Close the bread with both sides of
cream cheese facing each other.

Enjoy!

NACHOS

1 bag of tortilla chips
1 can refried beans
Shredded cheddar cheese
Mild salsa

Directions:

Cook refried beans until warm.

Place tortilla chips on cookie sheet-
enough for one layer with first covered in aluminum foil.

Place cooked refried beans evenly over chips.

Sprinkle desired amount of shredded cheese over the top-
bake for 10-15 min at 350° or until cheese is melted.

Top with salsa.

Enjoy!

STRAWBERRY WATER

Fun when served in a clear plastic like a Champaign glass or cup.

Strawberries (16 oz.)
Water
Ice

Directions:

In a pitcher, fill half way with ice.

Cut up clean strawberries (just cut in half and remove stem).

Pour in water until pitcher is full.

Place pitcher in refrigerator for 1 hour to chill and serve!

Ellie even likes to eat the strawberries
once she drinks the water.

Enjoy!

SNACK

Peanut butter creamy
Celery sticks

Directions:

Rinse celery and pat dry with a clean towel.

Cut off ends and cut each celery stick to make two sticks.

Take a butter knife and insert creamy peanut butter
into the curved part of the celery.

Enjoy!

SNACK

Green grapes
Sliced apples
Organic creamy peanut butter
Childs plate or paper plate with three separate areas

Directions:

Rinse grapes and apples.

Slice apples.

Place apples in the largest area.

Place peanut butter in one of the smaller areas.

Place grapes in the third area and serve!

Enjoy!

SNACK

Granola
Strawberry yogurt
Strawberries

Directions:

In a small cereal size bowl, place 1 cup of yogurt.

Top with 2 tablespoons of granola.

Take two clean strawberries and place on top.

Enjoy!

MEET ROGER

Age: 6/ 12 years old

Grade: 2nd

Eyes: Brown

Skin: Green

Favorite Color:
Roger's favorite colors are green and yellow.

Favorite activity:
Fishing, swimming, playing chess, and of course riding the yellow curvy slide at the World Famous Star School.

Favorite place to go on vacation:
Camping in a forest by a lake.

What does he want to be when he grows up:
He hopes to win a chess competition when he's older and would
love to be a forest ranger.

Pets: none.

Siblings:
an older Brother named Sam who is 17.

What school do you attend:
Star School.

Where we you born:
Grand Island, Nebraska

ROGER'S

FAVORITE RECIPES

SMOOTHIES

In a Blender:

1 cup of blueberries (rinse well)
1 apple (cleaned, cored and cut into 4 pieces)
1 orange (peeled and cut into 4 pieces)
1 cup of water
1 cup of frozen strawberries

Blend well and serve

Enjoy!

SMOOTHIES

In a Blender:

1 cup of red seedless grapes (rinsed well)
2 bananas (peeled and cut in half)
1 cup of frozen peaches
1 cup of water

Blend well and serve

Enjoy!

SMOOTHIES

In a Blender:

1 cup of peaches (rinsed well, cored and cut into 4 pieces)
2 bananas (peeled and cut in half)
1 cup of frozen peaches
1 cup of water

Blend well and serve

Enjoy!

ROLLED SANDWICH

White or Wheat Bread
Roast Beef Thinly Sliced
Romaine lettuce
Cream Cheese
Rolling pin

Directions:

Take a clean cutting board and cut crust off of bread.

Taking rolling pin and flatten bread as thin
as you can get without breaking.

Spread cream cheese evenly on top or bread.

Then place two slices of roast beef on top of bread
and place two cleaned romaine leaves.

Then grab once side of the bread and begin to roll.

You can then cut it in half or leave it
just like that and begin to eat.

Enjoy!

PASTA WITH VEGGIES

2 tablespoons unsalted butter
1 package of frozen vegetables (any mix)
1 bunch of basil
1/2 can of diced tomatoes
1/2 package of eggs noodles

Directions:

Prepare eggs noodles according to package instructions,
drain and set to side.

Microwave or cook veggies (follow directions of package).

Put butter into large pan and melt,
then add veggies and stir for about 3 minutes on medium heat.

Next, add can of diced tomatoes with juice.

Then add noodles and stir together on medium heat
for another five minutes or until noodles and veggies feel warm.

Transfer everything to a serving pan or bowl.

Take cleaned fresh basil leaves and clean scissors and
cut about ½ cup of basil and spread the fresh basil over the top.

Toss gently and serve. Enjoy!

BEEF BURRITOS

1 can of pinto beans
1 cup of Enchilada sauce (mild)
½ pound of ground beef
½ cup of shredded cheddar cheese
Tortillas

Directions:

Cook beef until brown; drain.

Drain pinto beans and add to ground beef in a pan

Add enchilada sauce and cheese

Heat tortilla and a roll it up with yummy mix inside
and you are all set.

TURKEY WRAPS

Butter lettuce
Turkey lunch meat
Sliced jack or cheddar cheese

Directions:

Rinse butter lettuce and pat dry with towel.

Place butter lettuce on clean plate curved side facing up.

Place two or three slices of turkey meat,
then one slice of cheese.

Then roll and eat with your hand.

Enjoy!

BAGEL PIZZA

Bagels
Pizza sauce or marinara sauce
Shredded cheddar cheese

Directions:

Slice bagels in half.

Place bagels on a cookie sheet, cut side facing up.

Use a spoon and spread marinara sauce
or pizza sauce evenly on each bagel.

Take the shredded cheese and sprinkle the
desired amount on top of the bagels.

Cook the bagels on 325° about 6 minutes or until cheese is melted.

Enjoy!

ANGEL HAIR PASTA AND TOMATOES

½ cup angel hair pasta
1 cup of cherry tomatoes
½ cup Basil
½ cup Vegetable Oil

Directions:

Cook a handful of angel hair pasta and set to the side.

Take rinsed cherry tomatoes and cut them in half.

Wash off basil leaves and cut into small strips with clean scissors.

In a pan, pour ¼ cup of vegetable oil,
then place the tomatoes in pan on medium. Cook
for about 5 min (flipping tomatoes often).

Then add basil and cook for a minute.

Then add pasta and another ¼ cup of vegetable oil
and cook together for two minutes.

Enjoy!

GRAHAM CRACKER SANDWICHES

Graham Cracker
Peanut butter
Bananas

Directions:

Take one graham cracker split in middle
to make two even pieces.

Spread peanut butter evenly on both sides.

Peel and slice banana and put four slices
of banana on the cracker

Take the other cracker and place cracker on top of the other.

Enjoy!

TRAIL MIX IN A CUPCAKE TIN

(be sure child does not have allergies to nuts before serving)

Peanuts
Almonds
Mini chocolate chips

Directions:

Mix and serve in a cupcake tin.

Enjoy!

YUMMY BLUE BERRIES

Blueberries 8oz.
Whip Cream
Cupcake Tins

Directions:

Rinse blueberries well.

Put in Strainer until fairly dry (about 30 min after rinsing).

Put cup cake tins on platter.

Place two cup cake tins together
(so they hold up better).

Place blueberries in cupcake a little less than half way. Top
with a small amount of whip cream and serve!

Enjoy!

YUMMY STRAWBERRIES

Strawberries
Powdered Sugar

Directions:

Rinse off strawberries and place on clean plate.

Put 1 cup of powdered sugar in a bowl.

Take the Strawberry and dip in the powdered sugar.

Enjoy!

MEET JESSICA

Age: 7 years old

Grade: 2nd

Eyes: Blue

Hair: White

Favorite Color:
Jessica's favorite colors are orange and red.

Favorite activity:
Drawing and sewing.

Favorite place to go on vacation:
Jessica loves amusement parks! She also likes water parks
and hopes to visit as many water parks as she can.

What does she want to be when she grows up:
Jessica loves little children and is hoping to be
a doctor for babies and little kids.

Pets:
None, but she likes to play with the neighbor's golden retriever,
Leo. The neighbors got Leo the same month that Jessica was born.
Jessica has grown up with Leo as if he were her own.

Siblings:
No siblings yet but she adores Joey's little sister and
is hoping her parents want to have a baby really soon.

What school do you attend:
Star School.

Where we you born:
San Jose, California

JESSICA'S

FAVORITE RECIPES

BLENDED DRINKS

In a Blender:

2 cups of watermelon (no skin, diced)
2 bananas (peeled and broken in half)
1 cup of crushed ice
1 cup of water

Blend well and serve.

Enjoy!

BLENDED DRINKS

In a Blender:

2 cups of raspberries (rinsed)
2 bananas (peeled and broken in half)
1 cups of frozen strawberries
1 cup of water

Blend well and serve.

Enjoy!

BLENDED DRINKS

In a Blender:

2 cups of nectarines (cleaned, diced, and remove seeds)
2 cups of apples (cleaned, diced and remove cores)
1 cup of frozen mangos
1 cup of water

Blend well and serve.

Enjoy!

SCRAMBLED EGGS WITH CHEESE

(Jessica knows people usually eat these for breakfast
but she likes them for dinner.)

2 eggs
2 tbsp. 2% Milk
1 tsp. chopped onion
1 tsp. of cheddar cheese
Butter
Orange slices

Directions:

Place pan on medium heat and melt a little butter.

Put the beaten eggs in the pan with onion.

Scramble together until eggs are fully cooked
then sprinkle the cheese on top.

Jessica likes to set the orange slices on the side of the plate
and eats them after she is finished with her eggs.

Enjoy!

COOKIE CUTTER PB & J SANDWICH

Wheat Bread
Peanut Butter
Strawberry Jelly
Any Cookie Cutter will do-
Jessica's favorite shape is a heart

Directions:

Take two slices of wheat bread-spread Jelly on one side
and peanut butter on the other side.

Put together and on a clean plate or clean cutting board,
press the cookie cutter down on the top of the sandwich
until the sides are cut.

Then you have it!
A heart shaped peanut and butter and jelly sandwich.

Enjoy!

CHICKEN WRAP

1 chicken breast
Pesto sauce
Romaine Lettuce
Cherry Tomato
Tortillas
Vegetable Oil

Directions:

Boil Chicken breast for in water with and 1 teaspoons
of oil for 20 minutes or until not pink in middle.
Let cool for 15 minutes.

Take one heated tortilla and place on clean plate.

Take 2 teaspoons for pesto sauce and spread
in the middle of the tortilla.

On a separate plate, dice up chicken and place
the desired amount of chicken on pesto sauce.

Next, place the cleaned romaine lettuce –
(about two leafs torn up) on top of chicken.

Then take clean cherry tomatoes and cut them in half
placing about five or six slices on the lettuce.

Now take one side of the tortilla and begin rolling.
And there you have it! A chicken wrap! Enjoy!

SPINACH SALAD

1 small bag or two hands full of spinach
8 strawberries
½ cup Feta cheese
1 Lemon

Directions:

Rinse strawberries, lemon and spinach
and pat dry with clean towel.

Place spinach on plate
(enough so you can't see the plate).

Remove stem from strawberries
and cut each strawberry into 4 pieces.

Place strawberries evenly over salad
about a handful for each salad.

Do the same with the feta cheese.

Cut the lemon in four pieces and
squeeze a few drops evenly on each salad.

Enjoy!

SWEET POTATOES

2 Sweet potatoes (fresh not canned)
2 tbsp. honey
Cinnamon (just enough to sprinkle on top)

Directions:

Scrub the Sweet Potatoes with a clean brush,
and then pat dry with a clean towel or paper towel.

Poke sweet potatoes with a fork at least 4 times.

Bake at 425° for 40 to 60 minutes or until tender.

Cut a "X" in the top of both sweet potatoes,
then use fork to open up.

Pour honey evenly on both sweet potatoes
and sprinkle with cinnamon.

It's super yummy! Enjoy!

EASY PEASY CHICKEN TACOS

Roasted Chicken (Precooked in store)
Corn tortillas
Finely Shredded Cheese (any kind)
Shredded Cabbage
Mild Salsa

Directions:

Heat the corn tortillas on stove top or microwave.

Place heated tortilla on plate.

Take desired amount of cleaned shredded cabbage
and place it in the middle of tortilla.

Next, take a couple of pieces of chicken without skin
and place in the on top of shredded cabbage.

Then top with cheese and salsa. About 1 teaspoon of each is good.

Jessica likes to make these with her family
because they are so easy to make.

Enjoy!

EASY CHICKEN SOUP

1 16 oz Chicken Broth
1 cup of diced Carrot
1 ½ cup of Roasted Chicken (precooked from market)
1 cup of diced celery
1 1/2 cup of egg noodles

Directions:

Prepare noodles according to the directions
on the package and set to side.

In a large pot, pour the chicken broth
and add the cup of diced carrots and celery.

Bring to a boil and turn down
to a light gentle boil for 20 minutes.

Bring to a low simmer and add cooked noodles
and 1 and ½ cups of diced chicken without skin.

Cook on low for another 15 minutes,
stirring every 2-3 minutes.

This is great on rainy days or right when Jessica
gets home from school.

Enjoy!

CHICKEN PASTA AND PESTO

3 tablespoons of vegetable oil
1 lemon
4 boneless, skinless chicken breast
(cut into halves then into strips about finger size)
for younger children cut smaller bite size pieces once cooked
3 tablespoons of pesto sauce
1- 8 oz package of penne pasta
Cherry tomatoes 8oz.
Parmesan cheese if desired

Directions:

Cook penne pasta according to its package;
rinse and set to side.

Clean and dice tomatoes and set aside.

Heat oil in large pan over medium to high heat,
then add chicken and the juice from 1 lemon.

Cook for 3 to 4 minutes on each side
(check to make sure chicken is not pink inside).

In a large pot, mix together pasta, chicken and pesto sauce.

Next, pour in tomatoes and cook together
on low for about 4 minutes, tossing occasionally.

Top with parmesan cheese and you are done. Enjoy!

BAKED POTATO WITH CHILI

2 Russet Potatoes
1 can of chili
Med Salsa
Shredded fine cheddar cheese

Directions:

Scrub potato until clean.

Rub a little vegetable oil on the skin of potato,
then sprinkle with salt and pepper.

With a knife cut an "X" on the top of the potatoes.

Place the potato in the microwave.

Most potatoes take 9-12 min on high.
Check to make sure it's soft.

Heat the chili in small pan.

Place potato on plate with "X" side up.

Open "X" with a fork, enough to make room for a ½ cup of chili.

Pour heated chili in space made in potato.
While chili is still warm sprinkle with shredded cheese.

Then top with salsa and you're set. Enjoy!

CRACKERS AND CHEESE

Wheat crackers
Sliced cheddar cheese (Cut each slice into four)
Cherry Tomatoes
Spinach (Raw)

Directions:

Clean tomatoes and spinach, remove stem
and cut in half then set to side.

Place six wheat crackers on a large plate,
then top the crackers with 1 spinach leaf,
1 slice of cheese, a slice of tomato.

Enjoy!

FRUIT WITH TOOTH PICK PLATTER

Fun when friends come over after school or to watch movie

Tooth picks
Apples
Banana
Strawberries
Peaches
Seedless Grapes

Directions:

Clean fruit, remove seeds from apples
and peaches as well as the peel from banana.

Cut into bite size pieces.

Place on a plate and insert a toothpick in each piece.

Enjoy!

MEET JOEY

Age: 7 years old

Grade: 2nd

Eyes: Green

Hair: Brown

Favorite Color: Blue

Favorite activity:
Baseball, baseball, and more baseball.

Favorite place to go on vacation:
Joey and his family have a list of all the major league baseball stadiums in the United States and Joey's favorite idea of a vacation is going on an adventure to see them each of them.

What does he want to be when he grows up:
A baseball player.

117

Pets:

A cat named Bonkers. They named her that because she does silly things like she growls like a dog when she sees a bird and she jumps on the lawn mower when they mow the lawn.

Siblings:

A little sister, Jackie, who is 4 years old.

What school do you attend:

Star School

Where we you born:

Austin, Texas

JOEY'S

FAVORITE RECIPES

SMOOTHIES

In a Blender:

2 cups of cantaloupe (no skin, diced)
2 bananas (peeled and broken in half)
1 cup of frozen mangos
1 cup of water

Blend well and serve.

Enjoy!

SMOOTHIES

In a Blender:

2 cups of apricots (cleaned, cored and diced)
2 bananas (peeled and broken in half)
1 cup of frozen mangos
1 cup of water

Blend well and serve.

Enjoy!

SMOOTHIES

In a Blender:

2 cups of figs (cleaned and diced)
2 bananas (peeled and broken in half)
1 cup of frozen mangos
1 cup of water

Blend well and serve.

Enjoy!

BREAKFAST BURRITO

2 eggs
2 tbsp. 2% Milk
1 cup of pinto beans
1 tsp. of cheddar cheese
1 tbsp. mild Salsa
Butter
1 tortilla

Directions:

Place pan on medium heat and melt a little butter.

Put the beaten eggs in the pan with onions and pinto beans.

Scramble together until eggs are fully cooked
then sprinkle the cheese and add salsa on top.

Heat tortilla and place it on a plate.

Take about a cup of the eggs and pinto beans
and place the mix in the center of the tortilla.

Roll it up and eat! Enjoy!

ROLLED CAPRESE SANDWICH

(Joey calls it "Crazy Sandwich" because when he was little that's
how he pronounced it)
White or Wheat Bread (tortillas work well too)
Tomato
Basil
Mozzarella cheese slices
Rolling pin

Directions:

Take a clean cutting board and cut crust off of bread.

Taking rolling pin and flatten bread as thin
as you can get without breaking.

Place cleaned basil evenly on top of bread-about 2 leafs.

Then take cleaned tomatoes and thinly slice. Add a slice of tomato
onto the basil leaves.

Last, take 1 slice of mozzarella and
place on top of tomatoes and basil leaves.

Then grab once side of the bread or tortilla and begin to roll.

You can then cut it in half or
leave it just like that and begin to eat.
Enjoy!

CHICKEN FAJITAS

1 pound of boneless skinless chicken breast
3 tablespoons of Vegetable Oil
1 can of mild enchilada sauce 8 oz
2 Red bell peppers
Tortillas

Directions:

In a large pot add water and 1 tablespoon of vegetable oil.

Boil chicken for 20 minutes or until no longer pink.

Cut chicken breasts into long thin pieces (finger size)
and set to side.

Take cleaned red bell peppers
and cut off stem and remove seeds.

Cut peppers into thin strips.
Place peppers into clean pan with 2 tablespoons of oil and
cook on medium heat for 5 or 6 minutes or until soft.

Next add the chicken and 1 cup of enchilada sauce
and stir together for about 6 to 7 minute on medium to low heat.

Place a warm tortilla on a plate and put about
two teaspoons in the middle of the tortilla.

Fold and eat. Enjoy!

PIZZA ENGLISH MUFFIN

Wheat or White English Muffins
Tomato basil marinara sauce
Shredded cheese (your choice)
1- 8 oz can of pineapple

Directions:

Preheat oven to 375°.

Place English muffin on a baking sheet with the cut side up.

With a spoon, cover the top of each muffin
with marinara sauce.

Then sprinkle on desired amount of cheese.

Lastly place two or three slices of pineapple on each muffin.

Bake for 8-10 minutes or until cheese is melted.

Enjoy

CHEESE SANDWICH

Wheat Bread
Sliced Mozzarella or Cheddar Cheese
Romaine lettuce
Tomatoes
Mayonnaise

Directions:

Take two slices of wheat bread place on clean plate

Put desired amount of mayonnaise on each slice

Place two cleaned leaves of romaine on bread
and two slices of cheese and slice of clean tomato.

Place the other slice of bread on top of the cheese
and you are ready to eat!

Enjoy!

WARM TURKEY SANDWICH

Wheat Toast
Turkey Lunch Meat
Tomatoes
Cream Cheese

Directions:

Clean and slice tomato then set to the side.

Toast the bread and spread cream cheese on each slice.

In a pan, on low heat, warm the turkey meat
(about two slices per sandwich)
for about 30 sec on each side.

Place tomato and turkey on toast and you're set!

Joey loves eating these with his grandfather,
who came up with the recipe.

Enjoy!

CHEESE & BROCCOLI BAKED POTATO

2 Large Russet Potatoes
2 cups of cut broccoli
Butter
Fine shredded cheddar cheese

Directions:

Cut broccoli—just tops—and wash.

Fill a pot with just a few inches of water
and insert steamer basket over the top.

Bring water to boil and add broccoli and
cover, lowering heat to a low simmer.

Cook broccoli for 4-5 minutes or until tender.

While the broccoli is cooking, work on potatoes.

Scrub potato until clean.

Rub a little vegetable oil on the skin of potato,
then sprinkle with salt and pepper.

With a knife cut an "X" on the top of the potatoes.

Place the potato in the microwave.

Most potatoes take 9-12 min on high.

Be sure to check to make sure the potato is soft.

While potato is cooking cut up the broccoli and place back onto steamer tray and recover to keep it warm.

Once potatoes are done, place them on plate with "X" side up.

Open "X" with a fork, enough to make room for the 1 cup of broccoli.

Place heated broccoli in space made in potato.

While broccoli is still warm, sprinkle with shredded cheese.

Sprinkle some salt and pepper and you're set.

Enjoy!

SLIDERS

Ground beef
Small rolls (cut in middle) or hamburger buns
Lettuce
Tomato
Ketchup

Directions:

Clean lettuce and tomato and set to side.

Take beef and roll into a ball, about size of golf ball.

Next, flatten the beef patty.

The patty should be fairly thin and round,
about the size of the bottom of a coffee cup.

Next, sprinkle it with salt and pepper.

Cook beef on medium heat for about 2 minutes per side,
or until not pink in middle.

Cut roll in middle and microwave for 20 seconds,
just enough to warm it.

Top your bun or roll with ketchup,
a slice of tomato and a torn lettuce leaf.

Add the cooked beef patty and you're set! Enjoy!

S'MORES

Graham Crackers
Mini Marshmallows
Mini Chocolate Chips

Directions:

**this might be messy so get ready to soak bowl
after or use a paper bowl.*

In a bowl, take one graham cracker and break it up
into tiny pieces, about the size of a mini marshmallow
(but doesn't have be exact).

Next place about 5 mini marshmallows on top of graham cracker.

Then take about 5 mini chocolate chips and place
those on top of marsh mellows, put in microwave for about
10 seconds, or until marshmallows expand just a bit

**be careful to not let it go to long or marshmallows
with explode and cause a huge mess in microwave.*

Next, take a spoon and mix lightly together.

Make sure it's cooled off and you are ready to eat.

Enjoy!

FRUIT ON A STICK

1 package of skewers
2 Apples
2 Bananas
6 strawberries

Directions:

Rinse fruit.

On a clean plate or cutting board, cut all fruit
Into pieces about the size of a quarter and as
thick as your thumb nail.

Place the fruit on in any order you like and eat.

Enjoy!

*Please note with smaller children, sand down
the sides of skewers ahead of time or closely supervise.*

SPRINKLEY BANANAS

(Super fun to make and super yummyJ)
Bananas
Mini chocolate chips
Creamy peanut butter

Directions:

Place package of mini chocolate chip evenly on a plate.

Next peel bananas
(about one banana per person and set aside).

Take one banana and a butter knife
and gently spread creamy peanut butter all around the banana.

Then, while holding the banana with your hands,
gently roll banana in mini chocolate chips.

Then place the banana in a bowl and slice in bite sizes.

Joey loves these for dessert!

Enjoy!

Thank you to Stacks in Campbell, California
for sponsoring this book.
Stacks is a business that not only provides amazing service
but also cares about the community
and I admire them for that.

Sincerely,

Julie Dart

STACKS

Michael Schmidt
Stacks
Director of Operations
314 El Camino Real, Redwood City, CA
& 139 E. Campbell Ave, Campbell CA
www.stacksbreakfast.com
michael@stacksbreakfast.com
www.facebook.com/stackscampbell

Made in the USA
San Bernardino, CA
12 October 2013